This book belongs to

TRADE MAXWELL SMITH

Jack and
the Beanstalk

RETOLD BY
Jennifer Greenway

ILLUSTRATED BY
Richard Bernal

ARIEL BOOKS

ANDREWS AND McMEEL
KANSAS CITY

Library of Congress Cataloging-in-Publication Data

Greenway, Jennifer.
    Jack and the beanstalk / Jennifer Greenway ; illustrated by
Richard Bernal.
        p.   cm.
    "Ariel books."
    Summary: A retelling of the classic tale in which a boy finds his
fortune at the top of a beanstalk.
    ISBN 0-8362-4903-8 : $6.95
    [1. Fairy tales. 2. Folklore—England. 3. Giants—Folklore.]
I. Bernal, Richard, ill. II. Title.
PZ8.G84Jac   1991
398.2—dc20   91-12376
[E]   CIP
                                                            AC

Design: Susan Hood and Mike Hortens
Art Direction: Armand Eisen, Mike Hortens, and Julie Phillips
Art Production: Lynn Wine
Production: Julie Miller and Lisa Shadid

Jack and
the Beanstalk

$\mathcal{O}$nce upon a time there was a widow
who lived in a tumbledown cottage with her
son Jack. Jack and his mother were so poor
that all they had was an old white cow.

One day when there was no food in the
house, and no money to buy any, the widow
said to herself, "I will have to sell our cow, or
Jack and I will surely starve."

So Jack's mother called him to her and said, "I want you to take the cow to market and sell her. But be sure you get a good price, for she is all we have."

"Yes, Mother," Jack replied, and he put a collar on the cow and headed to town.

Jack was delighted to be going to market by himself. As he walked he whistled a cheerful tune.

He was interrupted when he heard someone say, "You seem to be in a fine mood, young man. Where are you going today?"

Jack turned around. On the side of the road stood a strange little man. He was about four feet tall and dressed in a bright green suit.

"Why, I'm off to market," Jack said, "to sell our old cow."

"I'll buy your cow, if you'd like," said the little man.

"What will you give me for her?" asked Jack.

"I'll give you these magic beans," the little man replied. Then he opened his hand. Jack looked at the beans in the man's palm. They were all the colors of the rainbow.

"Magic beans!" Jack cried. "I've never seen any before!" And he traded the cow for the beautiful magic beans.

"Mother will be so happy," Jack thought, feeling very pleased with himself. Then he ran home as fast as he could to show her the magic beans.

But Jack's mother was not happy when she learned what he had done.

"Oh, Jack," she cried. "How could you be so stupid! You traded our cow for a handful of beans!" Jack's mother was so angry, she picked up the magic beans and threw them out the window.

Jack realized his mistake, but it was too late. The cow was gone and there was still nothing to eat for supper. Jack went to bed, feeling very foolish.

13

All night, Jack tossed and turned. "My poor mother and I will have nothing to eat tomorrow either," he thought miserably. "And it is all because of me and those magic beans!"

The next morning, Jack gloomily climbed out of bed. When he went to the window, he saw an amazing sight.

Where his mother had thrown the magic beans, a giant beanstalk was growing. It was thick and tall—so tall that it reached into the clouds!

"Mother, come quickly!" Jack called. And together they stood in the garden, staring in wonder at the beanstalk.

"I wonder where it goes," Jack said. "Perhaps I'll climb it and find out!"

"You'll do no such thing," said his mother. "Those beans have already caused enough trouble!"

But it was too late, for Jack had already started up the beanstalk. Up he climbed, higher and higher, until the cottage below looked no bigger than a bird's nest. Still, Jack could not see to the top of the beanstalk.

At last, Jack climbed through the clouds. There he found himself at the top of the beanstalk. A field of clouds stretched in every direction. In the distance, Jack could see an enormous stone castle.

He jumped off the beanstalk and walked toward the castle. Soon he stood before the entrance—a huge iron door. Not knowing what else to do, Jack pulled the bell. After a moment, the great door slowly swung open.

To Jack's horror, there stood a huge, ugly giantess looking down at him. Before Jack could run away, the giantess scooped him up in her huge hand. "Oh, good!" she said in a great big voice. "I've been looking for someone to help me with my chores."

Jack was so frightened, all he could say was, "Of course. What do you want me to do?"

"Well," said the giantess. "First you may help me light the fire and polish the boots. Now, we must be very careful when my husband comes home, for there is nothing he likes better than to eat roasted Englishmen for dinner!"

Jack didn't like the sound of that. But the giantess promised that she would hide Jack in the cupboard when her husband came. So he helped her light the fire and polish her boots.

All of a sudden, Jack heard a terrible
sound like the roaring of thunder.

"That's my husband," the giantess cried,
and she quickly hid Jack in the cupboard.
Then Jack heard a great booming voice:

Fe, fi, fo, fum!
I smell the blood of an Englishman.
Be he alive or be he dead
I'll grind his bones to make my bread!

22

And in stomped the giant.

He was much bigger than his wife and much uglier, too. He sat down at the table and shouted, "I smell an Englishman. Catch him and roast him at once!"

"Don't be silly," replied his wife. "That's only the mutton stew I've cooked for your supper." Peering through the keyhole of the cupboard, Jack watched her set down the biggest bowl of mutton stew he had ever seen.

23

The bowl of stew was so big that Jack could have sailed one of his small boats across it. The giant quickly ate the stew. He called for another bowl, and ate that too.

When he was finished, the giant said to his wife, "Now bring me the goose that lays the golden eggs." His wife brought a very ordinary-looking goose and set it before the giant. Then she went to bed.

After she was gone, the giant turned to the goose and said, "Lay!" The goose promptly laid an egg of pure gold. "Lay!" the giant said a second time, and the goose laid another golden egg. "Lay!" the giant commanded a third time, and the goose laid a third egg of gold.

Jack's eyes grew wide as he watched through the keyhole. "A goose that lays golden eggs!" he thought to himself. "Why, that would be a fine thing to have!" Jack wondered how he might steal it.

After a time, the giant's eyelids began to grow heavy and soon he fell asleep right at the table. He snored so loudly that the walls of the castle shook.

When Jack was quite sure that the giant was fast asleep, he crept out of the cupboard and tiptoed across the table. Then he snatched the goose that laid the golden eggs.

With the magic goose under his arm, Jack leaped off the table and ran across the stone floor toward the door. Just as he reached it, however, the terrified goose cried, "Help! I'm being stolen. Help!"

The giant awoke with a start. When he spotted Jack with the goose, he came racing after them!

"Stop," the giant shouted. "Stop, thief! Give me back my goose!"

But Jack didn't stop. He was too frightened to turn around. He kept running as fast as he could across the clouds to the giant beanstalk.

At last, he saw the top of the beanstalk. And still clutching the magic goose, he started climbing down the beanstalk. But he had not gone far, when the beanstalk began to sway violently.

Looking up, Jack saw that the giant was coming down the beanstalk after him! Jack began to climb down faster. The giant began climbing down faster, too. Just as the giant was about to catch up with him, Jack reached the bottom of the beanstalk.

He saw his mother standing by the cottage door, and he called to her, "Mother, quick! Fetch me the axe!"

His mother came running with the axe. Jack grabbed it and, with a single blow, chopped through the beanstalk.

With a great groan, the beanstalk came crashing down, and the giant fell with it. Now, where the giant landed no one knows, but Jack and his mother never saw him again.

Jack showed his mother the goose that laid the golden eggs, and she fed it some dried corn. The goose was so happy to be free from the giant that it laid a golden egg, then another, and another. Jack took the golden eggs to market and traded them for food and a new cow and much more besides.

And ever after Jack had climbed that giant beanstalk, he and his mother and the goose that laid the golden eggs all lived happily together.